CLEAR CUT

D1447499

MELODY DODDS

An imprint of Enslow Publishing

WEST **44** BOOKS™

Please visit our website, www.west44books.com.
For a free color catalog of all our high-quality books,
call toll free 1-800-542-2595 or fax 1-877-542-2596.

Cataloging-in-Publication Data

Names: Dodds, Melody.
Title: Clear cut / Melody Dodds.
Description: New York : West 44, 2020. | Series: West 44 YA verse
Identifiers: ISBN 9781538385142 (pbk.) | ISBN 9781538385159
   (library bound) | ISBN 9781538385166 (ebook)
Subjects: LCSH: Children's poetry, American. | Children's poetry,
   English. | English poetry.
Classification: LCC PS586.3 C543 2020 | DDC 811'.60809282--dc23

First Edition

Published in 2020 by
Enslow Publishing LLC
101 West 23rd Street, Suite #240
New York, NY 10011

Copyright © 2020 Enslow Publishing LLC

Editor: Caitie McAneney
Designer: Seth Hughes

Printed in the United States of America

CPSIA compliance information: Batch #CW20W44: For further information contact
Enslow Publishing LLC, New York, New York at 1-800-542-2595.

AUTHOR'S NOTE

Heather is a patchwork of people I've known who harmed themselves. I am one of those people.

YOU ARE NOT ALONE.

Our reasons were varied. None of us were suicidal.

One person, a boy, told me that he cut himself to drive the suicidal thoughts *away*.

I did it in order to feel something, because I'd been driven emotionally numb by the things going on in my life, and in my head.

YOU ARE NOT ALONE.

Others cut to stop feeling so *much*. So much pain, so much frustration, so much helplessness.

Some did it because it made the pain they felt inside a real thing, an actual wound that they could tend to and help heal. Still others did it to regain control.

There are as many reasons for self-harm as there are people who do it. And that's a lot—the CDC estimates in 2018 put the numbers at one in four teenage females, and one in ten teenage males.

YOU ARE NOT ALONE.

People don't typically cut because they are suicidal, but accidental suicides do happen. The emotional pain that leads to cutting can also lead to suicidal depression. If you are cutting yourself, you are **overwhelmed**. There is no shame in this.

YOU ARE NOT ALONE.
IF YOU OR SOMEONE YOU KNOW SELF-HARMS, PLEASE GET HELP.

Crisis Text Line
https://www.crisistextline.org/selfharm
Text 741-741

To Write Love on Her Arms
https://twloha.com/

S.A.F.E. Alternatives
https://selfinjury.com/

The Trevor Project (LGBTQ)
https://www.thetrevorproject.org/trvr_support_center/self-injury/

Befriender's Worldwide
Resources for people who self-harm and their friends.

https://www.befrienders.org/help-and-support-with-self-harm
https://www.befrienders.org/how-to-support-someone-who-self-harms

This book is for all the kids who try hard to help each other... even if the advice is bad.

Warning:
This book contains scenes depicting self-harm.

HEATHER WRIGHT –
ALWAYS ALL RIGHT

Through rain
    and snow
        and dark of night.

And never-ending
parent fights.

                                It's all good.
                                It's perfect.

I've got
Chairman Meow
to purr
    and cuddle.

I've got my best friend,
Liv,
to gossip
    and giggle.

                                It's fine.
                              It's terrific!

My parents yell
and I tell
    jokes about it.

DID YOU HEAR THE ONE ABOUT...

the lobster fisherman
who spent
all his money
on his wife's
college degree?

He was CRABBY
about it,
but at least
they didn't need to see
a PRAWNbroker!

And he *did* believe
that education
was SHR-IMPortant.

So he agreed
to going broke
by SHELLING out money
for everything
all those years.

But now,
his wife says
she thinks
that the lobsterman
doesn't do enough

and also
that he may be having
a SQUID-life crisis.

HOW ABOUT THE ONE ABOUT...

the bank teller
who made
all her own money.

Now that she's been working
at the bank
for a while,
she's LOST INTEREST.

> Not in banking,
> but in the lobsterman
> who put her
> through school.

She treats the lobsterman
like he's a LOAN SHARK
who wants to be paid back
in folded laundry,
        emptied trash,
                and clean litter boxes.

At work, she follows
        stock market crashes.
At home, she crashes
        the dishes.

> The lobsterman thinks
> the banker is
> "too big
> for her britches."

3

STOP ME IF YOU'VE HEARD THIS ONE...

about the parents
who never
stopped fighting?

One day,
the little girl asked,
    "How come
    you guys
    fight
            all
            the
            time?"

"Oh,"
they laughed,
"we're just practicing
for when
you're
a teenager."

                                    I'm
                            a teenager
                                  now.
                            But they
                              haven't
                              stopped
                              fighting.
                        And I'm just
                        a one-girl
                    stand-up show.

ONE NIGHT HE'LL CRACK

AND KILL HER.
AND PROBABLY KILL ME.

BEFORE DRIVING OFF
INTO THE NIGHT

WITH A BOX OF MATCHES
AND A CAN OF KEROSENE.

MAYBE TONIGHT!

These are things
    that I sometimes
        think think think.
    Can't stop thinking.

That's when
I need
to leave.

Can't go
out the front door
like a normal person.
    They'll suck me
    into their fight.

Your daughter this,
our daughter that.

My bedroom window!
It opens, but the screen won't
move, budge, get out of my way!

What do I have
that's sharp?
    A fork!

I stab the screen
until there is a tear
that I can fit through
        … almost.

EXTREME PAIN

shoots through
my arm.

Part of the screen
rips me open
from my armpit
to my wrist.

It   BURNS.

It   BLEEDS.

Just a thin line,
like a paper cut.

And it   HURTS

about that much, too.

How can such
a small cut

HURT   SO

MUCH?!

Except
it kind of
doesn't.
It kind of
feels   GOOD.

7

EXTREME CALM

That thin line
of blood is
weirdly calming.

I feel like
I'm watching
myself
        watch my arm
                bleed.

The heat
of the wound spreads
        into my shoulder
                and my chest.

My mind is clear
of chatter-thoughts:
        run or die, die or run...
Those are gone.

There is just the pain
pulsing with each beat
of my heart,
and a hush around me.

I feel all right.
For *real* for real.

                                As alright
                                as I pretend
                                to be.

EVEN OUTSIDE

I can hear
my parents
YELLING!

As I get to the end
of the driveway,

I hear
my mom
SMASH!
another dish.

> You'd think
> Lobsterman-Dad
> would buy
> paper plates!

So I
head to
Liv's.

LIV'S HOUSE

is the brightest
on the road.

Her mom makes ceramics.
All her little creatures
decorate the lawn all year.

Right now,
with Thanksgiving
in two days,
there are three turkeys.

Only right now,
I can't see
the turkeys.
Or the lawn.

Because right now,
parked in the driveway,
is an SUV.
White.
Shiny in the moonlight.
Not one I've seen before.

So I'm not
100 percent surprised
when someone
who is not Liv
answers Liv's door.

COOPER

Cooper Lessing
is not a person
I expect to see
at Liv's.

I can't even say
he's *the last person* I'd expect
because I don't expect him
at all,
for anything,
ever.

wealthy   middle class
spoiled   thankful
senior   freshman
moved here   born here
            hates Maine,   loves Maine,
                    especially   especially
                        the Mainland.

                    Wants to leave
                definitely   maybe
            for DC   for NYC
    to make bank in politics.   to work in theater.
                    These columns
                    don't
                    add
                    up.

BUT THERE HE IS

in Liv's doorway.

"Can I help you?" he asks.
Like he
belongs here and I
don't.

                              I can play this game, too.
                                      "Who are you?"

"C'mon, Heather.
You know.
I'm the
student body president."

                                          "Oh, yeah.
                                          Connor?
                                          Cory?"

"Cooper," he says,
and doesn't think
I'm funny.

                                          I try to
                                    shove past him,
                                    but he's big
                                    and heavy
                                    and doesn't move.

                        I open my mouth to...
                                          scream?
                                          yell?
                                    shout for help?

13

BUT THERE LIV IS

"Heather!"

She shoves him aside.
For her, he moves.

She gives me
a hug, then gasps,
backs away.
    "What happened
    to your arm?"

                I pretend
                I hadn't
                noticed.

                "Whoa!
                I should probably
                do something
                about this."

    "You know
    where the peroxide is."

                And I do.
                I know
                her house
                like it's
                my own.

There are
orange sodas
in the fridge
for me. (Liv doesn't drink it.)

There is
Raisin Bran
in the cupboard
for me. (Liv doesn't eat it.)

Furrgus,
her Maine Coon cat,
sits in *my* lap,
won't sit in hers.

I was more upset
than Liv
when her sister Paige
left
for Boston
in August
to start college.

And yet...

AND YET

I hear Cooper
through the bathroom door.

"How do you slice open
your whole arm
and not notice?"

I hear Liv:
"It's hardly a slice.
It's a scratch.
A deep scratch."

The peroxide

b   b l   s
  u b   e

but it doesn't
sting.

The "deep scratch"
still burns.
Hums.

It's not
soothing now.

It just hurts.

Like any
other cut.

AGAIN

I hear Cooper:
"It was her
whole arm.
How do you
not notice?"

                           "You don't know Heather.
                                 She splits firewood.
                                        Runs trails.
                                   Does archery.
                               She's not wimpy.

                         She's got a CRAZY cat.
                                She's always
                                    scratched
                                      and
                                  bruised
                                    at least
                                    a little."

"You're sure?
She's not one of those
crazy girls
who cut themselves
to feel better,
is she?"

                     What
                 is he talking about?

TURNS OUT

Liv
doesn't know
either.

She laughs.
"I don't know
what you're talking about.

So I'm going to
go ahead and say
the answer is
no."

"That's good.

Because
if she is,

you can't
hang out with her."

WHAT DOES *THAT* MEAN?

And what about it—
        his tone?
        how dad-like he sounded?
        the fact that he would say it *at all*?—
makes me so angry
that I'm shaking?

The cut
gives me an out:

        "This hurts a lot.
        I should probably
        go home."

                                Liv laughs.
                                "And what?
                                Have your *dad*
                                look at it?"

                        Because she knows
                                my parents.
                        Knows the fighting,
                                the yelling,
                        the *here-is-money-
                        go-get-dinner-from-Tideway.*

                And she knows
                they won't care
                about this cut.
                This deep scratch.

Cooper
doesn't know
any of that.

And I don't want him to.

I shoot
Liv a look
that tells her this.

She understands
exactly
what I'm saying
without saying.

To Cooper,
she says:
"Heather's father
hates the sight
of blood."

I grin and wink
at her,
meaning, *Nice save*,
then say,

"Good thing
he's not a cop,
like your dad."

Cooper makes
exactly the face
I was hoping for.

So I know
that he didn't know *that*
either.

LIV'S SISTER, PAIGE

is coming up
the driveway
as I leave.

She rushes at me
and gives me
an awkward hug
around the pizza
she's carrying.

> "Heather!
> Where are you going?
>
> You can't
> just leave
> already!
>
> It's not because
> of *this* jerk,
> is it?"

And she
PUNCHES
Cooper's truck!

My hero!

> "I cut myself,"
> I tell her.

Which doesn't really
explain anything...

She looks me
right in the eyes.
"Are you okay?"

I force
a laugh.

"It's only
a scratch."

It's not until
later

that I think maybe
she didn't mean
my arm.

IN SCHOOL ON MONDAY

Liv asks me
how my arm
is doing.

> She knows better
> than to ask
> about my Thanksgiving.

> She knows
>   the grands
>   come
>   down from Danforth or
>   up from Portland.
> She knows they
>   all stay
>   until Saturday.
> She knows they
>   fight, fight, fight,
>   fight, fight.

I ask Liv
how Cooper
is doing.

> Even though
> I already know.

> Because his SUV
> was back
> in the driveway
> on Saturday.

She blushes and
can't stop smiling,
so I know
I'm right.

I ask,
"How long
has this been
going on?"

She says,
"He just came over
to watch
some movies.

We're not,
   like,
dating!"

IN SCHOOL ON FRIDAY

When I ask
about
hanging out,

Liv tells me
she's sorry, but
she has plans
with Cooper.

*It's
a
date!*

And I want
to be happy
for her.

I really do.

But I'm really
       not.

WHEN I SAY *HANGING OUT*

I'm talking about
a project
we've been
working on.

Not a school project.

Sort of
        a "neighborhood watch" project.

A lot of our
"neighborhood"
is a forest.

This forest is (mostly)
pine trees.

They run
right to
the ocean.

We
        ("we" being Mainers
        in general,
        and
        people who live
        in our development
        especially)
are proud of our trees.

So proud
that we have
laws against
chopping
     them
          down.

                        Even if
               you don't get an
                   ocean view

                        unless
                      you *do*
                 chop them
                    down.

           Turns out,
         laws don't stop
          some people.

TWICE NOW

a new house
was built,
and before
it was built,
the plots were cleared.

It's so weird
to walk
to the water
down the same path
you took
only a week before,

and where trees
had stood tall,
to find nothing
at all.

No, worse than nothing.
    Stumps.
    Sawdust.
    Dead trees
      stacked
        like firewood.

Which is probably
what they'll become.

TRAIL CAM

Liv and I
were angry.

We wanted to know
who was doing this.

> My dad said it's
> > rich people from Away
> who don't have
> respect for Maine.

I borrowed
a trail cam.

The kind of camera
people use
to see critters
on their land.

Liv and I
were supposed to
set it up
this weekend.

Lucky for me,
it's a one-person job.

THE SNOW BALL

is what they call
our yearly
December dance.

Liv says
we should go.

I want to say
NO.

But I know
something is
up.

So I say yes.

DECEMBER
(SODA CAN TAB)

I open
a can of soda
  at the
Snow Ball.

    Liv is on the lookout
     for her
     "boyfriend."

I don't ask why
he didn't drive,
buy flowers,
or even ask her
to go.

    She sees him
     and starts to glow.
    Says to me,
     "Do you mind if I—"

"No.
I don't mind," I lie.

    So my best friend
    goes.

I tap
the sharp edge
of that soda can tab
against the soft
   inside
   of my wrist.

And it holds
a promise,

    like a kiss.

FRENCH KISS

Cooper,   Liv's *boyfriend*,
        acts
like he's surprised
to see her here
at this dance.

                                        She gets all
                                        doe-eyed
                                        and
                                        awkward.

I press the tab harder,
like a French kiss.

        And when he
        French kisses her
        on the dance floor,

I pull that tiny,
        jagged edge
across my soft
        uncut skin.
It makes an
        uneven tear
that bleeds
in dots.

A NEW FEELING

A burst of bright pain.

relief
release
calm
PEACE

I opened
myself.

Just like
I'd opened
the soda.

I slide the tab
into my pocket.

And right there,
at the corner
of the dance floor,

I do
an internet search

for that thing
Cooper said:

Girls
who cut themselves
to feel better.

LOVE, PEACE, AND
RAZORBLADES (LPRB)

comes up
as a vlog channel.

Something about
the LPRB girl
makes me
want to
keep watching.

She wears
a veil
to hide
her face.

I can only see
her lips, dark red—
  blood red.

Her hair glows
around her,
hanging almost to
her elbows.

As red as her lips
on the top,
then darkening
to black
at the
tips.

She could be
    12
or
she could be
    20.

She talks
for a long time.
It's too loud
to hear her.

The veil
    moves a little
as she talks.

The movement
    of the veil
and
    of her mouth
is calming.

Like the blood
is calming.

I subscribe to the channel.

DRAMA CLUB

is on Tuesdays and Thursdays.

Liv is
in here, too.

> Liv wants to
> work lights and sound
> on Broadway someday.

> I want to
> write and perform
> stand-up comedy.

The club
doesn't offer much
for writers.

But at least
the spring play
is a comedy:
> *Mapless, Maine.*

Liv used to talk
> about Broadway a lot.
Now she talks
> about Cooper, always.

She hasn't even asked
> about the trail cam.

CRITTERS

are all I've seen
so far
on the land
guarded by the trail cam.

I've seen:
      raccoons,
      squirrels,
      a big fat skunk,
      an opossum,
      some wild turkeys,
      a ten-point buck.

I even write
an essay
for my
creative writing class
about what I see.

Maybe
they haven't
sold this land.

Maybe
they won't.

And maybe
that skunk
will grow wings
and fly.

AT-HOME CIRCUS

Step right up,
    ladies and gentlemen!
But maybe keep the kiddies
    away from this one.

        See the Sideshow Parents!

Lobsterman-Dad
    hollers like a Nor'easter.
He can rebuild boats,
    fix and bait traps,
stay out
    after work
doing *Godknowswhat.*

              Bank-Lady-Mom
              does not bend
              in the storm.
              She can make dishes
              disappear—*SMASH!*—
              just like that.

        They don't cook!
        They don't clean!
        They leave all that to me.

        Well, why not?
        Every circus needs a clown.

HEATHER WRIGHT –
KEEPIN' IT LIGHT

It's not always easy,
believe me.

But when things get
      too scary,
I've got this notebook
      that I carry.

And I take whatever
they are saying
  (or yelling)
and try to
      make it funny,
spin it
      into comedy.

Try to
write a joke
about it.

                    Even when
            I'm broken inside.

Try to
be a funny
daughter.

                      Lately,
           it's been getting
                   harder.

HOLIDAY BREAK

Paige is home!

We are all
at the mall.
Like old times!
    Except my Dad
    didn't drive us.
    Paige can drive us now.
The mall is sad.
So many
closed stores.
And the Thrift Shoppe.

We buy
    makeup and underwear.
We try on
    crazy hats and boa scarves
    at the Thrift Shoppe
        and even find
        some stuff we like there.
We get
    just-OK pizza
    at the food court.
We use
    our gift cards
    and laugh a lot.

Until:
Liv
    spots Cooper

at the other end
of the food court,
with a girl
on his lap.

Paige says,
"Oh is that
his holiday
girlfriend?

His Bar Harbor
girlfriend?

His rich,
spoiled,
from-Away
girlfriend?"

Liv says,
"Shut up!
I'm sure she's
just a friend."

"Looks like
more than
just a friend
to me."

And Liv

THROWS HER SODA

at Paige.

CIRCUS AT THE MALL

Paige
        SLAPS LIV IN THE FACE.

"I will leave you here!"
        "I'll go home with Cooper!"

They're both swearing.

Cooper
and his group
of friends
all watch
the sisters
fight.

They all laugh
about it.

Even Cooper.

Paige stops yelling
at Liv.

Storms right over
to Cooper and
        KNOCKS HIS SODA OUT OF HIS HAND.

"You think this is funny?"
She swears some more.

ONE DAY SHE'LL SNAP

AND SLAP COOPER.
AND TELL LIV TO SHOVE OFF.
AND PROBABLY ME, TOO.

BEFORE DRIVING BACK
TO COLLEGE

AND NEVER COMING HOME.

JANUARY
(STRAIGHT PIN)

The Thrift Shoppe
still attaches
price tags
with straight pins.

My hands
    find their way
        into the shopping bag.
Find the tag
    and unpin it
        from the sweater.

Just holding it,
I feel better.

It's thin and cool.

I prick it
through
a pinch of skin.
    Then another.
        Then another.

Like I'm sewing.
Like a stitch.

A STITCH IN MY SKIN

that lets me
breathe again.

The pain is *sharp* and **hot**.

And I feel,
    as before,
        like I'm floating

above
everything.

Away
        from it all.

I can see only
tiny dots
of blood.
But they   HURT.

And nothing
around me
seems to matter
as much.
Things seem
like they're not even   REAL.

I feel all right.
I feel calm.
I feel   GOOD.

MIDWINTER BREAK

was always
Liv and me.

Snowshoeing
sledding
winter hiking
hot chocolate
warm blankets
movies

But this year,
I spend it with Sophie.

That's the LPRB girl.

She hides
her voice
just like
she hides
her face.

Uses auto-tune
or something.

It makes her sound
old and tired,
but also
somehow
wise.

It's as comforting
to hear
as it is
to watch.
The veil.
Her mouth.
That voice.

She mostly
just talks.

About cutting.
Cutting *herself.*

It makes her feel
the same as
it makes me feel:

better.

And I have to
admit that
maybe Cooper
was right.

COOPER

is the reason
  I am alone
    this winter season.

He made up
    with Liv
      somehow.

She told me
she wanted
to spend
most of the week
  with him
and asked
if I'd
  be mad.
I told her no.
And it's true.
I've got
something else
to do.
        Plus the trail cam
         and the critters.

Anyway,
I don't get mad.
She would just
get mad back
and then we'd be
    fighting.

FIGHTING

The night
we were at
the mall,
Paige came back over
to drop off
a bag I'd left
in her car.

Before she went home,
she asked me,
      "Is everything
      okay
      with you guys?"

                              "Yeah.
                              I mean,
                              we're not
                              fighting."

"Not fighting
is not the same
as okay."

            In my world,
            though,
            it is.

OR EVEN WORSE, NOT TALKING

The house is cold
from the silence
of my parents.

It's worse
than when they yell
at each other.

> *The merry-go-round*
> *has become a*
> *miserable-go-round.*

I wait.

For one of them
to say

anything.

Instead,
the silence hangs
around us
like fog.

Cold enough
to freeze the sun.

EARLY FEBRUARY
(TINY SAW)

Boxes of foil
have a metal
cutting strip.

It's basically
a tiny saw.

I snatch the box.
Sneak it
up to my room.

Set my arm
on the sharp little teeth
of that tiny saw
and *YANK!*

The pain
nearly makes me
cry out.

SAWED SKIN

My arm

BURNS

like a
skinned knee
and

BLEEDS

about the same.

It

HURTS

more
than last time,
but different, too.

The pain
carries me
like a warm breeze
and everything

JUST

spins under me
as I float away.

Everything
is okay.

No matter
what happens,
It'll be all

RIGHT.

DRAMA CLUB DROPOUT

That's what Liv is!

"It's just
too much,"
she tells me.
"I'm so busy."

                              "With Cooper?"

"Well, yeah!
He's going
away to college
in August.

We need to see
as much of each other
as we can
in the next
few months."

                              "Can you just
                              maybe come
                              once a week?
                              Instead
                              of quitting?"

          I hate how
          my voice sounds
          when I ask this.

            Like I
          might cry
          about it.

C IS FOR CONFUSED

I'M

truly confused.
I know
how things go
when Cooper is involved.
But still.

Drama Club
was a big deal
for Liv,
and I don't mean

KIND OF.

She's been
talking about it
since last year. I'm

STARTING TO

worry
about her future.
She's giving up so much
for this guy.
But I'm afraid
to say anything. I'd

HATE

to start a fight with her.

I just hope
he's not using

HER

like I think he is.

COMPETITION SUBMISSION

Mrs. Goode,
my creative writing teacher,
tells me,
          "I'm submitting
          the essay
          you wrote,
          'Lessons from the Critter Cam,'
          to the
                              Regional
                              Young Writer's
                              Competition.

          I'm allowed
                    to submit
          one freshman.
                    You're it!"
I wish
I had someone
to tell!

ACQUAINTANCES

This is a word
I learned
from Gramma Wright.

It's someone
you are friendly with,
but who is not a friend.

Someone
you don't
dislike.

Maybe you share
a sport
or a class.

I walk
down the hall,
and people wave,
say hello.

On the bus,
they don't trip me
or shove me
        or steal
                my book bag
        and play
                Keep Away.

No one calls me
a jerk
or the B-word.

The worst I get called
is quiet,
    weird,
        creepy,
            dorky.
And most of the time,
they're playing.

I have
dozens of
acquaintances.

CRITTER CAM

I read online
how to better set
the camera.

Sure enough,
I'm getting
clearer pictures
and seeing more.

> The raccoon
> > is getting f a t t e r.

> The skunk
> > has a family.

> The opossum
> > hasn't come back.

> There are too many
> > turkeys to count!

I could live here.
It's so peaceful.

I dream
about getting a tent
    and setting it up
    here on this lot
and calling this
home.

SPRING AND FAIRIES

I can hear
the circus
from the driveway...

              "You gonna just wait
                  for spring
            and let it melt?"

So I shovel.

"The laundry fairy
gonna drop off
clean clothes
anytime soon?"

Good one,
Lobster-Dad!
(This stuff
writes itself!)

I go inside
and start
the laundry, too.

Which makes
my mom
angry...

              "Our teenage daughter
                does everything!"

"Be proud
our daughter doesn't
run away from work."

"Sure don't!
I'm too lazy to run,"
I say.

I'm trying
to be funny.
But…

"You're taking
his side?"

"I'm not taking
any side,
Mom, I—"

"Go to your room!"

THIS IS IT!
SHE'S GOT A DISH!
SHE'S GOING TO
HURL IT AT ME!

I want
to try being funny
again.
But my mind
is blank.

SMASH!
"GO TO YOUR ROOM!"

I do,
but I grab
a piece
of that
broken dish
on the way.

(BROKEN GLASS)

The glass shard
is as big as
my hand.
I blow on it.

"I work,
Marilyn."

"Not that much
in winter, Lobsterman!"

I don't want
bits of glass
in me.

"We fix the boats."

"You put
a new engine in
last year. What's left
to fix?"

I carefully set the thin,
sharper part
against my arm
near the elbow.

"We repair
and build
the lobster traps."

"Oh, is that all
you do?"

SMASH!!   *SMASH!!*   *SMASH!!*

Just the coolness
of the glass
calms me.

"Gary's
getting serious
about the oyster farm."

                              "Gary who you drink
                              with after work?"

                    Yank!
                    No tugging.
                    It's clean and slick.
                    Blood flows
                    warm.

"Yeah. I do.
It's better
than coming home."

                    Like an ocean.
                    And, just like the ocean,
                    I am carried away,
                    weightless.

"It's

                              CUT

       better

                              CUT

            than

                              CUT

                 coming

                              CUT

                 home."

                              CUT

                              Home is where
                              the heart breaks.

SOPHIE SAID

in one of her LPRB videos
about how to
clean up
after a cutting event.

That's what
she calls them
in her newest videos.

She said
just use peroxide,
                    soap,
                              and warm water.

I did all that,
                then wrapped my arm
                        in gauze.

It was weird,
to do these things.

It made me feel
                like I was taking care
                        of myself
in a deeper way
                than just taking care
                        of my wounds.

It was like
mothering.

Only, I was
          the mom
          and
          the kid
at the same time.

There was something
          very peaceful
          about it.

I liked being able
to be kind
to myself.

I didn't have to
make any jokes.

I didn't have to
          lie to
the Me version
of my parent.

I was honest with Me.

> *You hurt yourself,*
> *and now*
> *I am going to help you*
> *heal and feel better.*

I felt like
          I loved myself.

I felt like
          I could be loved.

LIV NOTICES

Not the cuts.
I covered those.

The bandages.

I get
careless
with my flannel shirt.

"What happened
to your arm!"

I have already
made up
a whole story:
> "I was out
> in the brambles
> chasing Chairman Meow.
> *That* scratched me up.

> Then when I finally
> caught him,
> he was mad
> about it
> and wanted
> me to know."

"You should
just let
him go."

"I would miss him!"

"How could you?
He's so mean!"

I want
to tell her
that's *exactly*
how *I* feel
about Cooper.

But I figure
that will go over
about as well
as a fart
in church.

So, never mind.

LIV ASKED

Can I come
to Drama Club
just once a week?   They said okay.

Can I just
design the set?   They said yes.

She is designing
the set,
then handing it off
to the builder.

                            Meaning me.

                            I didn't get
                                an acting part.

                            And when your dad
                                builds lobster cages
                                and fixes boats
                                for a living,
                            you learn some stuff.

                            So they asked me
                                to build the set.

                            For some reason,
                                I said yes.

CONTEST NEWS

Mrs. Goode tells me,
    "You won
        second place!"

                                        "So I'm the first
                                              loser."

    "You came in *second.*
    In a *regional* contest
    with *hundreds*
    of entries.
    And you're
    a *freshman.*
    You should be
    really proud."

                                                  "I am!
                                When it comes
                                      to losing,
                                      I'm the very
                                            best."

She shakes
her head.
    "What is it
    with you kids?

    Anyway,
    there is a
    winner's ceremony
    and
    reading
    in two weeks."

READING?!

"Wait, WHAT?
We're expected
to READ?
Out loud?
In FRONT
of people?"

"The winners are
given
the opportunity
to
read their essay
at the awards ceremony,
yes.

You'll be
representing
the school, Heather."

I didn't get
an acting part
in a play with
19 roles!

Now they want
me to read.

How can I say no?

"Of course
I'll go."

THE SET

will be made
from cardboard.

Dad loaned me
a utility knife,
a heavy gray thing
     as big as a banana
     and twice as heavy.
There is space
inside the handle
to hold three blades.
     "Cardboard chews
     through blades," Dad told me.

Once I'm done
building the set,
     Dad will bring it
          to school
          in his truck.
I am in
the basement
     cutting cardboard
     like it's butter
          when the Friday Night Fights begin.

I figure,
    Great!
    More material!

But something's
    d i f f e r e n t.

MOM IS YELLING, BUT...

Dad is talking.
His voice
is even
and tired.

A low rumble.

                    I can't hear
                    his words.

Just his tone.

                                        Then Mom:
                                    "It's a marriage!
                            You don't get time off!"

Dad's
distant thunder
response.

                                        Mom again.

No rumble.

                    Heavy footsteps
                    to the front door.

                    Front door
                    opens.

                    Dad
                    leaves.

71

(UTILITY KNIFE)

Mom stomps
over to
the front door.
"IF YOU LEAVE
IN THAT TRUCK,
DON'T YOU DARE
COME BACK!"

I hear   Cool blade
Dad's truck   on warm skin:
start.   Hot rush!

He drives off.

And again.

Away   A wave
from   of
me.   calm.

And again.

relief
gentle peace

And again.

soft and
warm and
safe

*Like
a
trance.*

WARMTH

dribbles

d
o
w
n

  my
   arm

        Drip
      drip
         drips

       onto
     the
   basement
       floor.

      Bright red,
    so bright,
       so *much.*

Oh!
Oh, no.

FEAR

The utility blade
   is sharp and thick.

The cuts it left
   are **deep** and w i d e

         How will I hide this
            madness?

         So reckless.

                  Stop this bleeding!
                  Now *I'm* screaming.

HOSPITAL

The intern
    still has braces.
He gives me
    some side-eye.

                      I tell him
                      the same lie
                      I told Mom.

             "My cat...
             I was cutting cardboard...

        The third time he asks,
           my mom flips out.

          "My daughter
          is not a liar!
          And you
        don't know her.
       She's not wimpy.
     She's forever getting
          scratched
          and
         bruised."

                The same
                  excuse
                Liv used.

The intern nods
    and sends me
on my way
    with stitches and gauze.

DEAR SOPHIE,

If I am
  cutting myself
and think maybe it's
  out of control,

what's the best way to
  tell my parents?

Look forward to
  your (video)
  response!

Love and peace
  from the Most Northeast

THREE DAYS

Dad's been
away now.
I'm glad I'm busy
        with the set,
and practicing
        for the reading
and checking
        the trail cam.
                (There was a car
                on the property!)

So yeah,
        I've been busy.

Still, it's been
        impossible
                to sleep.

I GO TO LIV'S

Her mom
answers the door.

She tells me
        Liv is with Cooper.

She invites me in,
but I say no.
Thank you.

She says
        she hasn't seen me
        in a long time
        and she misses me.

                    This makes me sad
                    because these are things
                    I wish Liv would say.

DAY SIX

Something clicks.

Mom and I
fall into
a pattern.

The house
is quiet

but not
      tense,
      cold,
      awful
quiet.

It's
      peaceful,
      easy,
      comfortable
quiet.

It's warm and kind.

I like it.
      I feel
      guilty,
but I like it.

SET IS DONE

I text Dad
  and we make plans
    to get it moved.

I text him
most days,
and most days,
he texts back.

      But he is
       v a g u e
     with his answers.

          "Doing well."
         "Working a lot."

I text him,
  "SAME!"

With the trail cam
  and the drama club,
    plus now practicing
      for this reading.

I invite him
to the reading.

         He doesn't say
         either way.

THE READING

comes up so fast.
    I don't have time
        to be nervous
until I'm standing
    backstage
        at someone else's
        school.

The third-place freshman,
    a guy from Bangor,
is reading his essay
    about how
        his dog died
            on the same day
                his school baseball team
                    won the playoffs.
It *might* be a good essay.
    He's reading it
        so flat and mumbled,
            he may as well
                be reading
                    the obituaries!

The first-place freshman,
  Trey Neptune,
is back here
with me.
    Neptune is usually
    a Penobscot tribal name
    and he looks it:

He's got thick, dark hair
      and dark eyes.
High cheekbones
      and a broad nose.

He's tall and lanky
      and loose-limbed.
            His face
                  is kind and open.

Suddenly,
I am very
self-aware.

I am wearing
a *dress*.
      It's not even
            plaid.
      It's long-sleeved,
            and I left
                  the bandages on
                  underneath
                  (just in case).

Mr. Mumbly
      from Bangor
            finishes up.

MY READING

Next up is me!
And I read!
    About all the animals,
       and where will
          they go?

              We keep taking
               their land
              and when (*if!*)
              we give it back,
              it's been spoiled.

              Closed factories
              and brownfields,
              leaking pipelines,
              and forests cut clear...
I am careful
not to read too fast,
    to make it last
so they all get
    the whole impact.

And as I'm leaving the stage,
    I see Dad!
In the way-way back.

When I come off the stage,
Trey gives me
    a big smile.   "That was great!"

And I feel myself blush.

TREY'S READING

Even though
    he's been
        really nice,
I'm still
    kind of mad
        that I lost to him.

Trey calls himself
    a slam poet.
It sounds to me
    like a hip-hop artist
        with no music,
            only the rhythm
                of his poetry.
            The rhythm
                of himself.

It's called

                For Immediate
                Release
                (Native Boy
                Makes Good)

From the first line,
    it's so ironic
        and brave
that I'm instantly
    no longer mad
        about losing.

I'M SO IMPRESSED

that I wait
    backstage
        to tell him.

"I loved the words.
        And the performance!
            And the irony!
It was funny!
        But also serious in, like,
            the best way!"

                        He smiles at me.
                        "You have great
                        stage presence!
                        Are you going to
            Maine Theater Camp?"

"What's that?
I'm not a good actor..."

                        "You can be
                        a playwright!

                Maine Theater Camp.

            It's a day camp.

        Over summer.

    I'll be there.

    Look it up online."

85

SUMMER THEATER CAMP

A camp for Theater Dorks.

For kids who don't Sport.

Or actually camp
and hike or whatever.
Who do mind the weather.

Who aren't brainiacs either,
don't score well
at STEM.
(We think stars are pretty
but don't need to name them.)

For kids who CAN
write plays, build sets,
do tech, and perform.
Who all secretly plan
to take the world by storm.

Well, some
of that's me.
      Is all
      of that Trey?
Or is he
just like me,
looking for any
     excuse to play
     with words
     and be on a stage?

EITHER WAY

I ask
Mrs. Goode.

Mrs. Goode
is *thrilled*
about it!

> "I'm recommending you
> to this camp."

Recommending?

> "I'm telling this camp
> that you have talent
> and deserve
> to be there."

Well, hey!

I've never been told
I deserve anything
before.

At least not anything
good!

Ha!

DEAR MOST NORTHEAST

is not
how Sophie
responds.

But she does
respond.

She says,
"A couple viewers
  have asked me
    how to tell their parents
      about their cutting.
I would say…
…not to.

Do you think
they'll understand?

Really?!

  I have a friend
    who came out
      to her parents
        about her cutting.

      They threw her
      out of the house.

  I know someone else
    who went

to her parents
for help.

They locked her
in the psych ward.

Do you want
to be living
on the streets?

Do you want
to be locked up
in some loony bin?

No, you don't.

You want
to be free
and still have
a roof
over your head.

Keep your cuts and scars
        hidden.
Cut in places
        that can't be seen.

I cover this
in other
videos.

Take care
of your
cuts and scars.

Clean them,
        dress them,
                use cocoa butter
                on them.

I cover this
in other
videos, too.

                        Unless
                        you truly feel
                        like you want
                        to die,
                like you *actually* want
                to *kill* yourself?

I don't
recommend
telling your parents.

I just...
        don't see it
                ending
                        well."

I DON'T KNOW

about
    this
      advice.

I do know
it's
    not what
      I expected,

but it's
peaceful now
at home.

And I'm
healing.

And I
don't plan
to cut again,
    especially after
      what happened
        last time.

I decide to
(at least for now)
take
    this
      advice.

LIV FINDS OUT

about
Theater Camp,
and not from me.

She's *mad* about it!
"I can't
believe you!
You know
this is
my thing
and you
were going
to go do
my thing
without me?"

                                        "I thought
                                        Cooper
                                        was
                                        your thing."

Her face
squinches up.
"What's that
supposed
to mean?"

                                        I catch myself
                                        before I say
                                        something nasty.

"It's six weeks,
all day.
That's half
the summer
away
from Cooper.

I didn't think
you'd want to."

She pouts.
"You should
have asked me.

But I got
my application in.

Very last day,
but everyone
I talked to
says I have
a really
good chance."

And once again,
I *want*
to be happy
about this.

I really do.

But I'm really
not.

DAD COMES BACK

It's nice
to have Dad back.

Except it's not,
because
they are both
acting like
the other
is a scared
animal
or
a cranky
old person.

> *Walking*
> *on*
> *eggshells,*
> Gramma Wright
> calls it.

It feels
to me
like
  walking
    on
broken glass.

LATE MARCH
(TINY SAW)

They are
> not fighting
> (Mom and Dad).
They are trying
so hard
> to not get mad.

We are
> not fighting
> (Liv and me).
We are trying
so hard
> to be friendly.

All this
> not fighting,
all this
> *trying,*

  is so *trying*!

It's like walking
> through a field
knowing
> there are landmines.

> At least
> > with the saw,
> I control
> > when they go off.

The saw
    won't cut too deep.
        It brings fast heat.

The cuts raise
and burn
over the next
few days.

Every time
I feel my clothes
rake over them,

I get the same rush
                I am going
of being able
                to help you
to be kind
                heal and feel
to myself.
                    better.

APRIL

brings
      cold rain,
but also
      spring break.

Liv wants to hang!
      We go
      to the lot.

This is the first time
she's come with me
since I set
the first trail cam.

Dad gave me
another.
Liv and I hang it
in the cold rain.

Then we go back
      to her house,
          have hot chocolate,
          watch movies,
          eat popcorn,
          make microwave s'mores.
And for a few days,
it's like
it used to be.
      Until…

COOPER

has been
away.

He hasn't been
in touch.

      That's the reason
      Liv wants to hang.

We finally
kind of
get into a fight.

            She yells at me.

              "You just
                  don't like him!
              You've never
                  given him a chance.
              You should try
                  going out with us.
              You might even
                  have fun."

She's not wrong.

I don't
      like him
and I haven't
      given him (much of) a chance…

BUT HERE'S THE THING

He doesn't
like me
either.

And I'll bet
        my trail cams
that she hasn't
had this fight
with him.

I know she hasn't
stood up
for me.

Because,
when it comes
to Cooper,

Liv doesn't even
stand up
for herself.

TRESPASSING

I find the trail cams
      smashed to bits
in a nearby ditch.

      There are
          "No Trespassing" signs
          where the cameras were.

                    Dad tells me,
                    "These people
                    seem serious.

                    What you're doing
                    is dangerous.

                    I want you
                    to stay well away
                    from that land."

I think of my
      fat raccoon
      skunk family
      flock of turkeys
      missing opossum

and what
clear-cutting
that land
will do to them.

      My heart
      b r e a k s.

MAY
(TINY SAW)

N-O T-R-

                                            Lives
                                           I can't
                                           save.

E-S-P-A

                                          Things
                                         I can't
                                         change.

-S-I-N-G

                                          Feelings
                                         I can't
                                         control.

NO TRESPASSING

These letters
find their way
into my arm.

                A burning,
                bleeding
                eulogy

for the tiny plot
     of land
I stupidly thought
  would remain
    mine.

                The burn
              and the ache
              of my arm

isn't enough
to override

the burn
    and the ache
        in my heart.

Then I remember
    Sophie's words
        and start on my legs.

MAPLESS, MAINE

is a **huge** success.

I'm proud of the set,
even if it's simple.
It's sturdy.

Good thing,
because six
        different cast members
ran right into it
on opening night!

Even better,
it gave me ideas
for my own play.

Good thing,
because six
short weeks is all I've got
before I have to hand in the first draft
on opening day
of Theater Camp.

(I got accepted!)

LIV GOT IN, TOO

But when she calls me,
it's not
to celebrate.

"Cooper isn't
taking me
to the prom!"

                              "I hope
                          you broke up
                         with him then!"

"No,
he
broke up with
me!"

                                   "What?"

"I got mad
and he said,
FINE,
let's just
call it quits
right now."

                            "Why isn't he
                             taking you?"

"He said
it's not 'appropriate'
for him to take
a freshman

to the senior
prom."

                              I agree
                        with Cooper,
                            actually,

                        but I keep this
                          to myself,
                              obvi.

We walk
to Tideway and get
        ice cream,
        whoopie pies,
        chips,
        donuts,
        gummy bears.
Liv gets Moxie soda.
I get *orange* soda
because I am
        a sane person
                with working
                        taste buds.

It's hard for me
to see
Liv so upset.

                        Especially because
                          I am secretly
                              happy.

BUT ALSO GUILTY

Not just
about Liv.

Summer means
summer hours
for Dad.

He's up at 3:30
to meet the crew
at Dockside
for pancakes and eggs

before heading out
to pull and bait traps,
then clean the boat
on the way back.

It means dinner at 6:00,
in bed by 7:00,
to do it all over again.

It has been
        this way
since I can
        remember.
But this year,
        Dad's schedule
is testing
        Mom's temper.

She's not breaking dishes
        or even yelling,
but she talks
        through her teeth a lot.
I can see
        that it's killing her.

I feel bad
thinking it,

but sometimes
I wish

he'd go away
and be gone.

Not for *good*,
not forever.

Just enough to
recover

some calm
        and some peace
                and some quiet.

PAIGE IS HOME!

She shows up
     one night
when Liv and I
     are working on
          our stuff for camp.

Liv
has to
read a bunch
     of techie stuff
and design
     five stage sets.

I
have to
read five
     10-minute plays
and write
     one.

This may be
     the only time
          in history
we actually study
     when we say
          we are studying
          together.

LAST DAY OF SCHOOL!

Liv's mom
takes a half day
and brings us
for ice cream.

> Paige
> gives us each
> a tiny, tiny serving
> of champagne.

> > "To celebrate
> > not being
> > freshmen anymore!

> > You made it!
> > Congratulations!"

ALARM GOES OFF

the next Monday
and I'm not so sure
about this camp.

But I am ready
when Paige and Liv
come to get me.

My plays
      are written.

Liv's sets
      are designed.

               I feel
              for real
         like freshman year
          is behind us.

TREY

is the first person
I see
when I get out
of Paige's car.

He waves
at me.

I feel myself
blush.

He's got
that big,
warm smile.

I'm extra glad
        I wore
            a long-sleeved flannel,
even though
        it's too warm
            for long sleeves.

WEEK ONE

is a blur.
A flurry of
     reading,
     feedback,
     learning.

We read
and critique
each other's plays.

We four playwrights
keep away

from the techies
and actors.

They'd only
distract us,

and I'm already
distracted
by Trey.

MEANWHILE, BACK AT THE HOUSE

there is Dinner at 6:00
and Fighting at 7:00.
A flurry of
    blaming,
    complaining,
    defending.

        Mom looks to me.
        I look away.

Now that
    it's summer,
        I can
        just leave.
    I've always
        got somewhere
        to be.

MEANWHILE, BACK AT THE LOT

there's a TENT.

Next to that
is a kayak.

I stroll past it
        each evening,
but never see
        any people.
        Or a vehicle.

One night,
        I do see
a raccoon!

EVENINGS AT LIV'S

are like when
we were
in junior high.

Everything
is funny.
Everything
is fun.

Especially now,
        with Paige
                home.
There's always
        ice cream,
        soda (even if it's Moxie!),
        games,
        movies,
        laughter,
        talking.

I stay there
        overnight
                sometimes.

        One night
her mom
finds me
        in the kitchen
                real late.

I think
she's going
to be mad,

but she gets herself
a serving
of the cereal
I'm eating

and
tells me,

"You know, Heather,
you're always
        welcome here.
Even if Liv
        isn't here.
Okay?"

I feel
        embarrassed.
Wonder
        what she knows.

But I'm also
grateful
for this
kindness.

That someone   *I am going*
can be   *to help you*
kind   *heal*
to me.   *and feel better.*

WEEK TWO

is for revisions.
     Kind of like editing.

Rewriting
     what we wrote.

Applying
     what we learned.

My play is
sort of my essay
as a story.

Trey's play
is a poem   on feet,
          on legs,
     with arms
          and hands
              that reach
     and a voice
          clear and brave.

Trey's play
makes me
     want to
     write better,

and so
I do.

JULY FOURTH

Dad
doesn't
come home.

I don't have the heart
to leave Mom
all alone.

Even though
I have to

      turn down
      Trey's invitation
      to the reservation.

        Skip the parade
        with Liv and Paige

          and say no
          to their barbeque,
          too.

END OF WEEK TWO

Trey asks,

"Do you
want to go
get ice cream

    or something

        this weekend?"

ICE CREAM WITH TREY

We go
to Blueberry Hill.

I like
Jordan's better.
It's closer
to me.
          (I mean,
          by, like,
          seven minutes,
          but still.)
Plus Jordan's
has other food.

But Trey said
Jordan's
is too crowded
and loud,

and it was
his idea,
so I let
him pick.

He gets their
Maine Black Bear flavor,
which has little
raspberry-chocolate
bears in it.
          Groooss!

He probably likes
Moxie soda,
too.

I get
one scoop of
moose tracks
and one of
blueberry
        because
        I am
        a person with
        TASTE BUDS!

He laughs at me.
        "I like that
        you're funny,"
he says.
        "I like your play
        because it's funny,
        even though
        it's about
                something
                        serious."

SOMETHING SERIOUS

It doesn't feel
    all that serious
        to me.
Especially
    compared
        to Trey's play.

                    But it's rude
                    not to take
                    a compliment.

                    "Well, it's easy
                    to make it funny.
                    I mean,
                    it's about
                    silly animals."

Trey looks at me
with that wide, warm smile,
but there is something
in his dark eyes
that sparkles
with knowing,

He tells me,
    "The Penobscot
    have a lot
        of stories
        about animals.

Like why the raccoon
        is shaped that way
and why the loon
        sounds like that.

But also
stories of animals
helping people.

Not that we
deserve it."

He laughs,
but his face
gets a sad,
kind of faraway look.

        "Animals
        are important,"

he says
very seriously.

        "People
        forget that."

And I suddenly wonder
        if it's hard for him
to be around white people
        all the time.

WEEK THREE

We meet
the actors
and
the crew
     – lights and sound.

     Of course
     I already
     know Liv.

          I've heard rumors
          from her,
          but not much
          from anyone else.

Our plays
were turned over
to the actors
and the tech kids
first thing
in the morning.

While they
are reading
our stuff,
we are getting a crash course
in lights and sound,
set design and build.

I wonder
if anyone else
is as worried
as me.

Worried about
        if the actors
        and set designers
        and crew
                liked my play.

Worried about:
        will I like
                the acting
                the set designs
                the lighting?

Then suddenly,
it's after lunch
and it's time!

JOSIE

Sugar and hot sauce,
    this actress.

She's not afraid to
        TAKE   UP   SPACE.

Comes into the room
like a striped orange cat
    and has the hair
    to match,
        copper
        with platinum
        highlights.

Strolls to the back
        and talks,
        loud and proud.

Not afraid to
take OVER.

Sits on a desk
instead of a chair.

I'm thinking
there's something
    familiar
        about her.
    Is it her
    swagger?

THE FAVORITE'S FAVORITE

Josie
holds up
a script.

"Who
wrote this one
about animals?"

                                        I feel myself
                                              blush
                                    as I raise my hand.

Josie smiles.

                    It's like
                    the sun
                    comes out.

"I expected
a boy."

Josie laughs.

                    It's like
                    the birds
                    are singing.

She pops
her gum.

"Anyway,
your play
is my favorite."

ATTACKED

Dawson
is another actor.
    Spiked, bleached hair.
    Open, plaid button-down
    over a white T-shirt
    and oversized cargos.
Like it's
the early 2000s
or something.

Is that cool again?
I have a feeling
he decides
what's cool.

When I put my hand up,
Dawson
sees my arm.
The scratches.
The welts.

"What happened to you?"

                 I blush again,
              but this time
              with shame
             and anger.

Josie speaks
before I even
have a chance.

"She was attacked
by a raccoon.
It was very
traumatic.
She doesn't want
to talk about it."

And right there,
I know.
Josie is a cutter.

DEFENDED

I'm afraid
to look at Trey,

but it turns out
he already knew.

Later on,
he says,

> "Yeah, I noticed, like,
> the second day
> of camp.
>
> It's okay.
>
> I mean,
> It's not *okay*,
>   but it doesn't
>   scare me.
>   Or make me
>   think you're crazy."

I look at him now
and see
    for the first time,
    really recognize,
the deep sadness
in his eyes.

"BUT LISTEN,"

Trey says.
"Have you talked
to someone?"

                              "No. I mean, sort of…"

"Do you plan to?"

                                        "No.
                              I was told not to."

Trey raises
an eyebrow,
but does not ask
by whom.

"Do you have someone
you *could* talk to?"

                              "No, not really."

"I'll give you
the name
of a counselor."

                              "I don't think
                              I'll need it.
                              I think
                              I'll just quit."

"I don't think so."

                              "How would you know?"

131

"I have a cousin ...
I *had* a cousin."

Oh.

Trey whispers,
"Do you want
to kill yourself?"

"No."

"Have you ever
wanted that?"

"No.
I almost did
by accident
and it scared me."

Trey takes
        my hand
and gives me
        his smile.

He is so kind
        and relaxing.
I want
        to tell him
                everything.

I want him to say,
        *You can talk
        to me.*
But he doesn't.

He doesn't,
so I can't.

BETRAYED

Liv finds out
    somehow
        and she freaks.

    "Cooper
    was right
    about you!'"
Her eyes
    are wide
        and scared.
She is
    afraid
        of me!

                I tell her
                the same lie
                I told the young MD.

                "Cooper
                was right about
                Chairman Meow.
                He jumped on me...
                and you know,
                he gets out."

Liv gives me
    no side-eye.
She *wants*
    to believe.
The ER sent me home.
    Who is she
    to disagree?

END OF WEEK THREE

Josie asks me,

"Do you
want to go
hang in Bar Harbor?

    Or whatever?"

BAR HARBOR WITH JOSIE

We go for
    ice cream,
    coffee,
    lobster rolls,
    blueberry pie!

We take selfies
with the human-sized,
ice cream-loving
lobster
outside of Ben and Bill's.
Then Josie
goes in and spends
FIFTY DOLLARS
on candy.

We take a
two-hour cruise
on a giant boat
where they let you
handle the sails.

We go in
all the dumb,
basic
tourist-trap shops
    that my mom hates
        because they are owned
            by people from Away.

The ones my dad tells me
        to stay out of because
                they are staffed by
                        college-aged boys
                                from the Russian Mafia:
                                        all tattoos,
                                        spiky hair,
                                        wolfy smiles.
Josie
smiles back
and she
FLIRTS
with these
        frightening,
        exciting
        young men.

If Josie
were a boy,
I would want
to date her.

        If Josie
        were a boy,
        my parents
        wouldn't *let*
        me date her.

                Luckily,
                Josie
                is a girl.

WEEK FOUR

is rehearsals.

The actors are
"moving off book,"
meaning
trying not to use
the scripts.

The playwrights
yell lines to them
when they forget.

Except this playwright.

I am (once again)
building sets.
It's cool, though.
Trey is impressed.

They are also making us
fill in
some of
the acting rolls
when four actors
is not enough.

(Also Dawson
has to play
        a girl in one,

which he
        is totally cool with,
        which makes me
like him more.)

Overall,
        we are
                cruisin' along.

CRASH

I am asleep
on Liv's couch
and rudely awakened
by a knock
on the door.

Who the...?
Cooper!

Liv
        comes flying
                down the stairs.

Already ready.

Hair up,
makeup.
Things she usually does
in the car.

"Don't be mad," Liv says,
"Paige is still
taking you to camp."
                                "Are you even coming today?"
"Of course," Liv says,
        but her
                reddening face
        says
                something else.

HERE IS WHAT I *THINK*

You could
have told me.

You literally
had all night
to tell me.

You could
have woken me up
and been like,

> *Hey,*
> *I know*
> *you're my best friend*
> *and everything*
> *but my*
> *MEAN*
> *EX-BOYFRIEND*
> *WHO HATES YOU*
> *is picking me up*
> *in the morning, so...*

But here is what *I* say:

"Um, okay."

GONE

At camp,
      Liv is not the only
            one missing.
      JOSIE is gone,
            too.
Trey
      is outside
            in the sun,
working
with the cast.

I
      am inside
under bright lights,
working
alone on sets.

With a
utility knife.

Smaller
than the one
I screwed up with.

This one
is thin
and orange ...
How much
damage
could it do?

JULY

(SMALL UTILITY KNIFE)

I make a quick,
light cut.

It's a rush.

Like a drug.

I bet this
is how
addicts feel
when the pills
kick in.

I make
     another one
     and another
until my side fills
     with slices
and my sadness
     is eclipsed
          by real,
          raw,
          physical

                    pain.

DITCH CLASS

My phone
buzzes.

It's Josie!
"Ditch class
and meet me."

It's not class,
      it's camp.
I asked
      to be here,
and it
      cost money ...

but wouldn't it
      show Liv
a thing or two?

SWIM

We ride rented bikes
to Lakewood Pond.

Since it's midweek
and before noon,
    there is almost
        no one
            here.

Josie strips off her
    leggings,
    tank dress,
      long-sleeved camisole.
Underneath all that
is a one-piece
swimsuit.

I don't notice
much about
the swimsuit.
I am
    stunned,
    dazed,
    amazed
by her skin.

SKIN

Josie's scars
    are like
        a city map.
One that includes
    the subway
        below the roads.

They are thick
    and in layers,
        like a pile
of sticks
    before
        the bonfire.

Like a pile
    of bones.

     I am   I am
       horrified   relieved
       fascinated   nauseated
       mesmerized   disgusted
       terrified   soothed

     Is this
what I look like
      to
                Trey
                Paige
                Liv
                ?

AFTER SWIMMING

"I swam
in junior high," Josie says.
"Now, it's all about theater.
I'm a triple threat!"

She can
      sing   "All that
      dance   and a bag
      act   of chips!"

She is
trying out for
America's Got Idols
in the fall.

"If I don't
get discovered,
then it's college.

Chicago
or New York.
Then I'll light out
for Cali

and chase down
my fame.

What
            about
                    you?"

WHAT *ABOUT* ME?

"This theater camp
is the closest
    thing
    I'm going to find
       to a comedy class
         in Hanworth, Maine."
Which makes
    me wonder:
why Maine
    for Josie?

Why not
    summer theater
       in New York
         or Boston?
I look
    at Josie's skin
       again,
and think
    I know
      the why.

    But I ask her
    anyway.

      And the story   she tells me
      is ugly.

THEATER IN MAINE

was Josie's
punishment.

"My parents
made me come
up here
for the summer
     with my dad,
     who's working
     on a house.

I was *supposed* to be
in Boston
with my brother
     who will be coming home
     from his final year
     at West Point
for the first half
of summer.

But I got caught
cutting
at school.

My parents
     didn't take it
          well.

My school
     pulled me out

of art class
for counseling.

They made me
eat lunch
in the principal's office.

My friends
all pretended
they hadn't
known.

Everyone
made me feel
    like
    a freak.
        Like a
        time bomb.
            Like I was
            dangerous.
When
what I needed
    was
    kindness.

I'm telling you:

Don't talk
to adults
about cutting.

It won't
end well."

JOSIE = SOPHIE = LPRB

I've heard this story.
A longer version.
From a veiled face.
    "*...was*
      kindness

        To feel
        loved.

        To feel
        heard.

        And also
        just to feel.
        Any *kind*
        of way.

        About
        anything.

        Because feeling
        so bad
        for so long
        made me numb.

        That's why
        I started cutting
        in the first place."

BACK AT CAMP

Liv is here
She came at lunch.
"I told you
I was coming!
Where were you?"

Josie tells her,
"We did
some one-on-one work
on Heather's script."
Then she drifts off
to find the other actors.

"So what, is she
your girlfriend now?
I don't care
if you like girls,
but not *that* girl."

"Why not
that girl?"

"Because *that* girl is bossy
and full of herself!"
Then she storms off
to find the other techies.

Trey says,
"*I* think
that Josie
is all an act."

ONE DAY

Josie and I spend
every free moment together.

I'm the only person who
gets her.
She's the only person who
gets *me*.

Then one day,
Josie asks,
"Can you hang?
        Like, spend the night?
Or I
could come home to you!"

        No way
        can she come
        to my place!

        My parents
        embarrass me
        sometimes even
        to Liv.

        No way
        can a stranger
        see how I live.

                I tell her,
                "Maybe
                tomorrow."

TOMORROW

Josie asks again,
about me staying
overnight.

But I have
no way
to get there.

"We'll get you a car."

I don't know
what that means.

"An Uber.
Like a taxi,
but less smelly.
Usually."

"Is your dad
okay
with this?"

"My dad
went back
to Boston."

ALONE

Josie says,
    "I'm alone
    in this house
    my dad 'finished.'

He works
for a company
that builds these
monster houses
for really, REALLY
rich people.

    They build
    in places
    they aren't
    supposed to.

        My dad
        is their lawyer.
        He makes
        all of that
        okay.

        He also 'finishes':
            He hires decorators
            and landscapers
            and people
            to stock the pantry.

It's a job
he loves.

But then,
in my family,
        love is
                a maid, a cook,
                a canopy bed,
                private schools,
                down comforters,
                my own bathroom.

I'm not
complaining...

        But to my parents, love is not
                time,
                attention,
                talking,
                laughing,
                sharing meals,
                playing games.

I thought,
since I'm alone,
maybe
we could hang.

Like sisters!"

THE CAR

Josie got us
pulls up
    outside
    my house.
Josie is inside the car
with a weird look
    on her face.

Turns out,
her dad's
giant mansion
    with the trees
    that were cut down
    illegally
is in
my
development.

We drive
    down the hill,
        down another,
            toward the water.

Trees line the road.
You'd never know
there was a house here.

But there is a gap   with an eight-foot gate,
        where Josie
        enters a code.

THE HOUSE

is all stone and white plank,
    all peaks and dormers.
Black shutters decorate
    tall, arched windows.
It stretches
    in either direction
from a main door (painted red).

Inside
are spiral double staircases,
    marble fireplaces,
    ceilings as high as the sky.

It's beautiful.

Inside
are 10 bedrooms,
    12 bathrooms,
    a servant's kitchen.

The true front of the house
    is all windows and more windows.
They all face
    the ocean.
Of course
    they do.

Between the house   and the ocean
    is a lawn.
    A LAWN.

Where there used to be
HOW MANY SQUARE FEET
of pine forest?

Clear cut
down to
nothing.

There are not even
any stumps.

It's horrible.

I CAN'T STAY

I tell Josie this.

I try
        to explain
                that this house
        is everything
I hate.

I show her my arm.
"Half of this,"
I point to the lawn,
        "is because
        of things
        like that."

                "Really?
                Half?

                It's not because
                of your parents?

                Or kids
                at school?

                Or your
                best friend
                who's
                abandoned
                you?"

I MEAN...

"I can't deal
with adults
right now!"

"Let's just
go stay
at my house."

"My dad's
going to bed
in an hour.

And my mom
probably has
work to do.

They'll leave us alone."

"No, they won't!

They'll want
to know:
*Who's your
little friend?*

*And why's her hair
that color?*

*And why's she
dressed like that
in the middle
of summer?*"

"YOU CAN'T LEAVE!"

"I wear
long sleeves
all the time
and they never
ask me
anything."

"I'm not going.

I can't deal
with grown-ups!

I'm having
a really hard time
right now
and I just
need you
to stay."

I am in
over my head.

Josie needs help
that I don't know how
to give her.

How can you
help a girl
whose father
is 300 miles away,

and left her alone
in a 5,000-
square-foot house?

Suddenly,
I am *desperate*
for my parents.

I don't care
how much
they yell.

"Let me
just call
my mom real
quick and let
her know
we're coming."

"I swear
if you don't
put down
that phone

I will kill
myself
right here
in front
of you."

WHAT CAN I SAY?

"I'll stay."

4:00 A.M.

I know because
I always wake up
when my dad leaves.

But it's not him
waking me today.
It's Josie.

I hear a car outside
and her voice.
But by the time
I get to the main entrance,
she is in the car,
and the car
is at the gate.

I check my messages.
Just before she left,
she texted me:

*"I'm going
home."*

JOSIE IS GONE

I stare
at my phone.
    There's no way
    Josie would do this.
This is nonsense!

                Leaving me here
                in this giant house
                all alone.

If only I hadn't
    fallen asleep.
Or we'd gone
    to my house.

           I'm going
           home.

I will probably never
see Josie
again.

What if
    she's dead?

          She was the only
             person I had!

I need
    to tell somebody!

Who to tell?

I don't know
    who needs
        to know.

Desperate,
      I text Josie,
"Are you
      coming back?
What
      about the plays?"

             If she doesn't answer,
             I'll tell Paige.

I start packing my things.
I feel hollow,
      like when my pet rat died
        in seventh grade.

             I realize
             I am *grieving.*
             But I'm not sure
             exactly what
             (or who?)
             for.

THE POLICE

find Josie
in the locked bathroom
of a Bar Harbor cafe.

She had cut herself
      from wrist
          to elbow.
      from knees
          to groin.

Her blood
      seeped
          under the door.

I FIND OUT

when they come
     to my house.

No disco lights.
No siren.

Just two men
in uniform.

All apologies.

     "...her last text."

          "...Intensive Care..."

    " ...ambulance..."

            "...just in time..."

"...father was notified."

When the officers
     are gone,
my parents:

     "What haven't you told us?"

          "What do you know?"

WHAT DO I KNOW?

I   admit
that Josie and I
were at the house
alone.

"DON'T   worry
about getting
in trouble," Mom tells me.

"Yes," says Dad.
"Just please
tell us
everything you

KNOW."
I tell them
about Josie
being left
by her dad.
But I don't say

ANYTHING   about the cutting.

Josie's
or
mine.

AT THEATER CAMP

Mom said I could skip, but I wanted to come.
A counselor (Ms. Turner)
is here. A psychologist.
   To talk to us
   one-on-one
   about Josie.

                                   I'd rather talk
                                          to Josie,

                                   so when it's my turn
                                             I decide
                                                to ask
                                       if I can see her.

The counselor is older,
and pretty,
and looks
a little sad.
   "I spoke
   with Josie
   this morning," she tells me.
                                       "How is she?"

"She asked
to speak with me—"
                                       "Is she okay?"

"—about you."
                                          "What?"
                  "Heather,
                   please.
              Roll up your sleeves."

MY WORLD SPINS AWAY

I feel
like someone
ice-bucketed
me.

But also
like I am
on fire.

     I want to
          scream   die
          confess   cry.

I am
          ashamed   by
          betrayed   for
          exposed   of
          saved   from

my
          deep
          dark
          dirty
secret.

          I roll up my sleeves.
            I pull up my shirt.
              I even describe my legs.

THINGS YOU CAN DO
INSTEAD OF CUTTING

Ms. Turner's list
is ridiculous:
> listen to loud music
> jump rope
> chop wood
> snap a rubber band
>> against your wrist
>
> tie a red string
>> around your wrist
>
> use a red marker
> hold an ice cube.

But Ms. Turner seems so
> hopeful
> optimistic
> honest
> kind...

that I promise
to try.

WEIRD FEELING

I'm kind of waiting
   to feel
like cutting

so I can see if
I can make myself
   not feel
    like cutting.

TREY SAYS

"Probably *I* should have
told someone.
But I would have felt
like a snitch."

Paige says,   "Is this
                      over a boy?
                      Because I
                      will kill him!"

Liv says,   "...but how could I know that?
                      Cooper said
                          girls who do that
                              are nuts,
                      but you're not.
                          You're my friend."

Liv's mom says,   "Remember
                      when I told you
                      you're always welcome here?
                      You still are."

MY Mom says   "Honey, I'm sorry,
                      I'm so sorry,
                      so sorrysorrysorry..."

DAD SAYS...

goodbye.

Ms. Turner
    had to tell them.
        The law made her.

They met
    more than once,
my parents
    and this counselor.

They decided
our house is
        toxic
    divided   unhappy
      a trigger.

So now,
    Dad will just visit.

DAD PROMISES...

that our development
is suing
Josie's father.

    And will identify
    other plots
    with a high chance
    of being
    clear cut.

    These plots
    will then
    be guarded
    and monitored.

    Like I did.
    Only better.

    He tells me
        who to talk to
    to make sure
        I'm part of the team.

He promises,
    and I believe him.
Because back in May,
    he didn't even promise.
And he still came
    to see me read.

THE PLAYS

get produced
in spite of
everything.

And people come
to see them,
even Cooper.

I end up
taking
Josie's roles,

which is weird
but seems right.
    (Even though
    she hasn't
    been in touch
    to ask.)
The acting coach
was all about it.
    "I don't know why
        they didn't send you
           to the acting track.
    I guess
        you'll just have
           to come back."

THE HARDEST PART

may be the scars.

    No amount
    of cocoa butter
    can hide the fact
    that I'm a cutter.

        "You *were* a cutter,"
        Ms. Turner
        corrects me.

    She says to
        accept that I did it,
            but to think
                of cutting
                    as something I
                        used to do.

    A phase.
        Like ketchup sandwiches,
        or blue hair…

"Or a bad tattoo
that I later regret?"

        "Some people actually
        cover those scars
        with tattoos," she says.

                "But you didn't
                hear that
                from me." *Wink, wink.*

TREY AND I

are having lunch
the last day
of camp.

      "I've got
      a lot
      of stories
      about animals,
      if you ever want to,
      like, call me
      or anything."

              Dawson
            wanders past us
           "Ohmygod, dude.
              Kiss her
              already!"

      Trey's smile
      goes crooked
      and his face
      gets bright.

Probably not
as bright as mine,
though.

                   "What kind
                   of stories?"

MAMA BEAR

"Well, like
there's one
about this bear.
There's this little kid
who gets trapped
in a cave
and left
to die
by his nasty
stepfather.

But Gluscabi—that's our
Great Chief, right?
Our protector?
He sends
his little buddy
Porcupine
into the cave
to help.

Porcupine, like,
glows his eyes
at the kid
and somehow
that calms him down."

"Really?
I'd freak out
more."

"Right?
Anyway, Porcupine
calls out to all the forest critters
to come move
this boulder.

And they all show up!
Like it's a party
or something.

Wolf,   raccoon,
caribou,   turtle,
possum,   rabbit,
          squirrel,
        and too many
        birds to list.

Most of them,
why even bother?
Maybe they were
placing bets
or something.

Of course,
they all try,
and they all fail,
and a lot of them
get hurt.

Then finally,
this Mama Bear
shows up and
moves
the stupid rock."

IS THAT IT?

"I feel like
there's more."

"There is."

"What's the rest?"

"It's really long."

"You don't
remember."

He shakes his head.
      "I better relearn
      this stuff.
      I'm Native.
      I'm supposed to be
      All Wise
      or some nonsense."
He pauses,
like he's
deciding something.
      "I was just thinking,
      you were kind of like
      Josie's bear.

      Like, all the other animals tried,
      but only the bear
      could free her.

      But then,
      you're kind of like
      the kid, too.

      And Ms. Turner
      is your bear."

I finally
can't help it.
I start laughing.

"I know.
It's a mess.

Plus, my dad's
going to kick my butt
if he finds out
I forgot all this stuff!

But I think
you were good
for Josie.

I think
you helped her.

And I'll
bet she's glad.

Someday,
            somehow...
she'll let you know."

THE OTHER HARDEST PART

We have been working
     on my "triggers."
          Things that make me
          want to hurt myself.

I say: **Ms. Turner translates:**

my parents fighting   lack of security

     Liv's   feeling
SUCKTASTIC   left out or
   "boyfriend"   "isolated"

clear cutting   lack of control

in my development   "climate anxiety"

          What?
     This work sucks!

                         Ms. Turner says
                         I need to be aware
                         of my triggers
                         when school starts.
                         She also says
                         I have to tell people
                         what I think
                         and how I feel
                         for *real.*

(RUBBER BAND)

Ms. Turner's list
actually helps.
I've gotten most
of my "triggers"
under control.

But sometimes
I want
an outlet.

SEPTEMBER (Red Marker)

Ms. Turner and I
have talked
about being scared,
feeling helpless,
having no control.

OCTOBER (Chop Wood)

We have talked
about wanting
to die.
Feeling suicidal.

NOVEMBER (. . .)

I don't want to die.
I was never suicidal.

DECEMBER (. . .)

I am not Josie.
I was never Josie.

I could have been.
But I got lucky.

THE SNOW BALL

Our yearly
December dance.

Like last year,
Liv wants to go.

She has a date.
        A *real* date.
He is taking her
for dinner
before the dance
and he
        (well, his dad)
is driving.

I have a date, too.
Liv told Trey
about it
        (of course she did)
and he asked
if he could take me.

So I said yes.

JUST LOVE & PEACE

When he called
about the dance,
     Trey asked me
     about Josie.

I've been afraid
     to check,
but tonight
     I decide
       it's time.

LPRB has a new name:
           JLP
There is just one video.
     I press play.

There is Sophie,
     but with no veil
     and no voice effects.
There is Josie.

     "Hi. You guys
     know me
     as Sophie, and I am.
       (It's short
          for Josephine.)
     Except from now on,
       I'm Josie.

A lot of the advice
that Sophie gave you,
I've learned
it was bad.

I spent the summer
in this magical place
and made this
great friend and...
          screwed up bad."

Josie starts crying,
but calms herself.

          "Listen:
          I said before
          not to tell your parents.
          That was wrong.

          I'm saying today:
          Find someone,
          any one person
          you can trust
          and talk to them.

          Let them help you.
          When you get
          good help,
          it feels amazing.
          It's the biggest relief
          in the world,
                    even
                    better
                    than
                    cutting."

LOVE, PEACE, & HEALING

I wonder
    if Josie
    will be okay.

    If this will be
        for her
    like it was
        for me:
            a phase.

    Something
    that we will
    look back on...
        I don't think
        we will laugh.

Even seeing
her scars,
I didn't understand
    that her pain
        ran so deep.

    Can a person
        ever
    escape that?

I like to think so.

I like to think
she'll learn to cope
and maybe even
get famous!

I hope
she does.

I open
the comments
and leave her
a note:

Dear Josie,
We hurt ourselves,
and now
someone is going to help us
heal and feel better.

Love and peace
from the Most Northeast

WANT TO KEEP READING?

If you liked this book, check out another book
from West 44 Books:

THE VANISHING PLACE
BY THERESA EMMINIZER

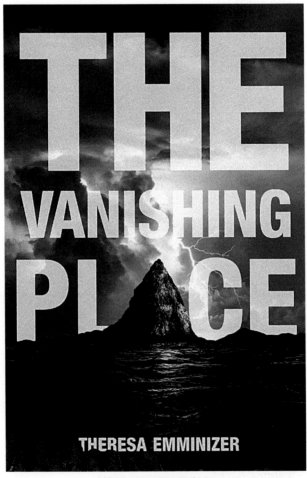

ISBN: 9781538385081

It Started

with a *yes*.

A *yes*
that slipped
easily
from my lips.

*Would you girls want to
        meet up later?*

        We could all go out
on Nate's dad's boat?

Jay's green eyes
were both
        nervous and eager.

His voice was
low and soft.

        Like the moon

                s u s p e n d e d

over the water.

A small doubt
like a mosquito
tickled the back of my neck.

But it was carried away
by the sweet-smelling
air of the deep blue Florida night.

Moonlight
gives me courage.

But Eva looked unsure.

Don't worry, Jay laughed.
    You girls will be safe with us.

We're locals, remember? He winked.
    We know what we're doing.

My excitement
was like static electricity.
If anyone touched
my skin,
their hair
would stand
on end.

Yes! I squealed.

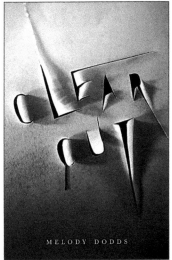

ABOUT THE AUTHOR

Melody Dodds is a chemist and former substitute teacher. In addition to this book, she is the author of another verse novel, *Little Pills*. She shares her home with two cats and one husband, and is building a foil ball exclusively from candy wrappers. It is currently the size of a small pumpkin.